THE ELI DIARIES

Book Two

Skin Deep

by

Melody Carlson

Published by Amaris Media International

ISBN: 1975812107
ISBN-13: 978-1975812102

CHAPTER ONE

Everyone betrays me. That's just a fact of life, and why I trust no one. Because eventually they'll mess me up—both figuratively and literally. That's why I keep my heart to myself. And why I felt blindsided when my heart went out to someone else for a change. I'd call this 'someone' a friend, but that's overstating things. He's just this weird guy from school . . . Eli Shepherd. Sure, he's been somewhat friendly to me, but that's not so unusual. Most guys (the straight ones anyway) can get real friendly. At least at first. But they just want a piece of, well, *action.* Because even though I'm new at Kennedy High it seems my 'reputation has preceded me.' It figures. But back to Eli—I wasn't prepared to actually care about this dude or anyone for that matter. But somehow I got caught up in the moment.

For some reason, I felt compelled to go down to the Surf Shop yesterday. Okay, I just wanted to talk to Eli. He'd been doing so many weird things lately—I just wanted to know what was behind it all. At least that's what I told myself when I walked down there. But it wasn't long before Eli and I were interrupted by his brother totally flipping out, yelling for Eli to get into the house. And, fine, I took a hint and headed for home.

A few blocks away, I heard sirens blaring and honking—and a couple of EMT vehicles raced down the street. But when I saw them pull into Eli's driveway, I turned around and went back. By then several curious neighbors were gathered on the sidewalk. And a tall surfer dude told me that Joey Shepherd had just suffered a bad heart attack.

"One of the good guys," Surfer Dude said grimly. "Best surfboard shaper on the West Coast. Ya know him?"

"Sort of." I didn't admit that I'd been dreaming of getting one of his boards or that I knew his son Eli.

"Man, it'll be a bummer to lose him."

"Do you think he'll die?" I asked.

"I heard it's pretty bad." Surfer Dude shook his head. "And he's got all those kids too."

After awhile, Eli and his weirdly large family emerged from the house, clustering together in the front yard. They were all sobbing and hugging, and it didn't look good. After a few more minutes, the paramedics wheeled out a gurney. I couldn't see much through the crowd, but Surfer Dude nudged me. "Looks like he didn't make it," he whispered. That's when my heart betrayed me by softening. I felt bad for Eli.

But when I tried to express some concern, which was pretty awkward, Eli seemed sort of preoccupied. I mean he was obviously sad—I could see tears in his eyes—but it was like he was distracted. He told me he had 'things to do,' which made no sense. What was there to do? I mean besides cry or scream or kick something? But as the EMT truck slowly drove away, with no lights or sirens, Eli turned to me with a strange expression. He told me to 'buckle in,' and that it was 'going to be a wild ride.'

Okay, I get that he was probably in grief—maybe even in shock—but even so that was a pretty bizarre thing to say. I really didn't get it. But then again . . . Eli is an oddity. No one really gets him.

The next day, not to be out-weirded by weird Eli, I decided to do something else totally out of character. I used some cardboard and felt pens to make a sympathy card. Then I 'borrowed' some flowers from a neglected planter outside of our decrepit apartment complex and walked them over to Eli's place. But the closer I got to his house, the stupider I felt. And that's when I heard that voice — the one that plays through my head sometimes. I'm sure it's just me, being all negative and hopeless, but I call it the *voice of doom.*

You're such a loser! Are you seriously going to knock on his door? Hand over those lame tokens of sympathy? And then say what? You're pathetic, Maggie! Do you really want him to laugh in your face? You should know better!

I was about to chuck my snitched blooms and beat it when I saw Eli wave to me from his yard. Realizing there was no turning back, I put on my brave front, which I'm pretty good at, and continued toward him like this was completely normal.

"I know this is kinda lame." I handed over my sad little gifts. "But I just wanted you to know someone cares."

"Thanks." He stared at the card and flowers with such intensity. Like I'd handed him the keys to the castle.

Finally he looked back at me. "This means a lot to me, Maggie."

"Well, uh, I know what it feels like to lose a parent," I mumbled.

"I know you do."

I blinked then tried to conceal my shock. How could he know that? But, really, why should I be surprised? Eli was always doing and saying weird stuff. It's just his way.

"Do you miss your mother a lot?" he asked.

I shrugged, trying to act natural. "Well, not like when I was little. I guess I got sort of used to it. You will too . . . in time."

His eyes lit up. "And I'll see him again too."

I waved a hand. "Yeah, right. If you believe that religious bunk."

Eli seemed to study me closely. But not the way most guys look at me, running their eyes up and down, smirking in way that always makes me feel naked . . . and later ashamed. Eli stared straight into my eyes, like he was trying to see something in there. Looking so deeply I felt worse than just naked—I felt exposed clear down to my soul. And I didn't like it.

"Maggie," he spoke quietly, "what would your mom do if she could see you now?"

"What do you mean?" I shoved my hands into the pockets of my cutoff jeans, fighting the urge to swear at him.

He tilted his head to one side with a hard-to-read expression. "What do you think she'd say to you?"

"Just what are you getting at?" I suspected he was about to lay into me about my skanky reputation. Not that I've ever heard him get down on anyone else before. But something about Eli always feels like he's got all the answers up his sleeve—and yet he holds back like he doesn't want to play his cards. It's confusing. Instead of answering, I just glared at him, wishing I hadn't attempted to do something *nice*.

"I just wonder, Maggie. Would your mom be happy for her little girl?"

That did it! "First of all, I'm *nobody's* little girl," I snapped. "And second of all, my mother was a junkie who didn't give a—" I stopped myself from using a foul word. "My mom didn't care about herself *or* her little girl." I wanted to scream that my mom died of a freaking heroin overdose—and that her poison had been supplied by my step-dad, who's now doing time in Salano. Instead, I locked eyes with him. "But you probably knew *that* too. I suppose everyone in this neighborhood knows all the dirt on me by now." I shook my head, wishing I'd never met this jerk and hating myself for getting pulled in. "So much for a fresh start at a new school!" I growled.

"A fresh start?" His brow creased like he wasn't sure what I meant by that.

"Yeah." My tone grew snarky. "Is English your second language? A fresh start is like a do-over, a clean slate. Duh!"

"Something deeper than just a make-over?"

I rolled my eyes at him.

"Because I don't think you can really change the outside of your life without changing the inside, Maggie."

For no rational reason I wanted to slap him hard or spit in his face. I wanted to scream and swear and lash out. To let loose all the anger bursting at the seams inside of me. But I kept my hands in my pockets, balled into tight fists, and I simply glared daggers at him. And without saying another word, I turned and walked away.

Forget Eli! I don't know why I let myself care about him in the first place. Note to self: don't do it again! But as I stormed back home, I could hear that voice of doom again, laughing at me.

I told you so, loser. Maybe next time you'll listen.

CHAPTER TWO

As I sat in the chair across from my court-appointed therapist, I seethed in silence. It didn't help that Gloria had just handed me a little black notebook, insisting that I should write in it 'at least once a day.' Is she for real?

"Think of this as my prescription, dear. It'll help you get well." She smiled like this was a good idea.

Trying to conceal my extreme aggravation, I resisted the urge to check my phone and see how many minutes were left in this long painful hour of 'counseling.' "What am I supposed to write?" I asked in my usual therapy patient monotone.

"Write about your true feelings, Maggie. I promise that you'll feel better when you put it down on paper." She droned on in her saccharine sweet voice. "It'll allow you to see what you're going through with fresh clarity. And someday you'll look back at your journal entries and perhaps even laugh." Okay, this convinced me that Gloria really does live on Planet Delirious.

"I doubt that I'll ever think my life's humorous." I ran my fingers over the smooth black cover, imagining setting fire to it, watching it melt and burn. "But even if I wanted to, uh, write . . . I wouldn't know where to start."

"Start with your friends and family and—"

"*Seriously?*" I shook the book at her. "You mean those liars, cheaters, haters, betrayers? You think I'll feel better if I write about all that crap?"

Her pale brows arched like she'd made some headway with me. "Is that how you see the people in your life, Maggie? As liars and betrayers and whatnot?"

I wanted to scream 'hell yes,' but simply nodded, wishing I'd kept my mouth shut and hearing the voice of doom hissing at me, saying I'd blown it.

You went too far, Maggie, said too much. You'll be sorry. Just blow this joint, get away before it's too late. Gloria is out to get you! Do not trust her!

"I'm well aware that you've been hurt a lot in your life," Gloria spoke quietly. "But you never seem to want to talk about it. I thought writing might help you to open up. Can't you give it a try?"

I glanced at the door, considered bolting, then simply shrugged.

"The problem in your other school was related to how you relate to boys," she pressed on, "More specifically, the sexual relationships you were involved in, Maggie, and the problems relevant to those relationships. Would you care to talk about that?"

"So . . . I slept around," I said nonchalantly. "No secrets there. Most kids my age sleep around."

"Do you still have, uh, *casual* sex?"

I wanted to ask what she thought was 'casual' about it, but simply shrugged.

Gloria leaned forward and, removing her reading glasses, peered intently at me. "Maggie, how do you *feel* after a casual sexual encounter?"

"Feel?" I frowned.

"Do you feel happy and contented? Do you feel loved?"

I rolled my eyes. "Get real."

"Do you feel respected afterward?"

"*Respected?* You mean for being a great *lover* and giving a guy a good time?" I laughed so loud that I actually snorted. "Yeah, right."

"You're an intelligent young woman, Maggie. I think you know what I mean."

I narrowed my eyes at her. "Don't be so sure of that."

She picked up her pen and shook it at me. "Maggie, you need to respect yourself." Her sweet tone suddenly turned firm. "If you don't respect yourself, you can't expect anyone else to."

"Yeah . . . right." I feigned a yawn.

She cleared her throat. "Anyway, I think you'll find that journaling is a wonderful way to explore those feelings. And like I said, I expect you to write something every day." She returned to her oblivious monologue. "Perhaps you can start your journal by answering this question. Why don't you respect yourself? And remember, lying to your diary is like lying to yourself. So keep it honest." She checked her watch, the signal that we were done. I tried not to roll my eyes as I faked a smile. Shoving the stupid black notebook into my bag, I hurried outside. As I passed a trash bin, I heard that voice again.

Stupid, stupid, stupid! Gloria's an idiot and so are you if you listen to her! Throw that hideous book away — right now! You don't need Gloria or her lies. And if you believe her moronic prescription for happiness, you're a bigger fool than I thought.

CHAPTER THREE

Yet, a few hours later, I found myself sitting in my stale little bedroom, madly penning my pathetic feelings — using a Motel Six matchbook for a bookmark just in case I need to torch the evidence. But I'm not journaling because I trust Gloria's professional expertise, or even Gloria personally. The only reason I wrote anything in this stupid book was because I *need* that moronic woman's help. Without a therapist's sign-off, I'll get kicked out of school. It's not that I love Kennedy High, but after being expelled from SHS last May (long story and not my fault!) I suspect this could be my last chance.

Why do I care? Sometimes I wonder. But here's the deal, despite my *don't-give-a-damn* façade, I have to agree with

Gloria about one thing. I am intelligent. I'm a closet-academic who desperately wants go to college. I'm convinced that my brains and looks are my only ticket out of this crap-hole of a life—and I plan to use them to the max. I'd use just about anything—or anyone—to get a better life. And why shouldn't I? It's obvious that no one else can help me.

My incarcerated step-dad used to make promises to me in his letters . . . but he eventually gave up. After I told him he was dead to me. And, really, why should I believe him? After all, Rod isn't really my dad. I have no idea who my "real" dad might be. I'd known several by the time Rod came along. And the truth is Rod had been the closest thing to a real dad. Well, until he killed my mom, which he claimed was an accident, but the court claimed was manslaughter. But it's not like Rod can help me anyway. By the time he gets released from Salano, I'll be close to thirty and, if all goes well, I'll have finished law school and be earning the big bucks as well as some respect as an attorney by then. I won't need anyone. In fact, I don't really need anyone right now.

Not even Grams. Even though I've lived with my maternal grandmother these last few years—after some unfortunate and unspeakable stints in foster homes—I know I can't expect much from the old lady. Oh, she loves me—at least she says she does. But it's obvious that she loves Jack more. Jack Daniels that is. All you have to do is keep an eye on our apartment complex dumpster on any Sunday night to know that's true. I used to be mortified when Grams dumped a week's worth of empties. Like I thought the whole world was listening to the clang-clang-clang of breaking glass, but now it just reminds me to get my homework done for Monday. No big deal.

But I have to give Grams some credit. She might be a hot mess, but she does give me a room and sometimes, like after the Social Security check comes, there might even be food in the fridge. And no one sexually abuses me here. Not without my consent anyway. But that's about all I can count on here.

I learned long ago that the only one really taking care of me is me. And I've found my own ways to get money. Gloria says I'm resourceful. Some teachers have called me manipulative. And jealous loser chicks with zitty faces and flat chests call me a slut. But that's an exaggeration. Just because I sleep with a guy and he gives me a few bucks does not make me a prostitute.

Anyway, the sooner I get out of high school and blow this joint, the happier everyone will be. I just hope I can hang on that long. I'm only a junior . . . and graduation feels impossibly far off. Especially considering that the school-year's barely begun and I feel like it's already getting dicey. Seriously, it's like half the kids at Kennedy want to kill me — and the other half (males and lesbians) just want to sleep with me. Seriously, what's a girl to do?

I pause from writing and find myself thinking about Eli again. Okay, I told myself I wouldn't write about that weirdo in my journal. But it bugs me that I can't wrap my head around the things I've seen him do. Giving that Goth dude lunch money was one thing, but that bit with Savannah's dead dog — and I was sure he was dead — well, that was just seriously whacked. What's up with him anyway? And why do I keep obsessing over him. It's not like I want him for my boyfriend . . . or do I?

Of course, this reminds me of Terrence Stuart. He pursued me so hard when Grams and I moved here in the summertime. Terrence acted all protective at first. And even though he's not much to look at, I appreciated the attention he gave me . . . at first. But now he assumes he's my boyfriend, which is such a joke. Sure, he's good for a free ride to school or a cheap meal, but I'm not ready to be tied down to him or anyone. Besides being a total narcissist, Terrence is a bully. It didn't take long before he started to act like he owned me, like I'm his personal property. Get real, dude!

Just last week, Terrence got rough with me . . . and I know it'll just get worse. Note to self: *part ways with Terrence ASAP*. Being paired with that lowlife is like trying to surf with a rusty anchor tied to your ankle. Time to lose the loser and his broken-down junk-heap of a pickup too! It feels good to have made up my mind about Terrence, but now I'm thinking about Eli again.

It took me about a week, but I got over being ticked at him for bringing up my mom that day. I'm sure I overreacted. Because really, he's not so bad. He's a lot better than Terrence. He treats me lots better too. And his interest in me has been flattering. Even so, it's not like I want to sleep with him. At least I don't think I do.

I think my interest in Eli is more about curiosity than attraction. The dude is just so freaking weird. Seriously, every time I turn around it seems like he says or does something that totally messes with my head. Maybe that's a good thing because it helps me to keep a safe distance. And I'd be a fool to make myself vulnerable to him — or any guy. I've learned my lessons — hurt them before they can hurt you. If you don't give your heart away, no one can stomp on it.

CHAPTER FOUR

By Monday morning, my plan to dump Terrence Stuart was neatly in place. I'd ignored his texts and calls all weekend, except for late last night when I accepted his offer of a ride to school this morning—my chance to dump him face-to-face.

I usually try not to take the coward's way out, that's just one of my standards. Thanks to my less than lily-white reputation, no one expects me to have any standards, but I do. Like no sexting—only an idiot with no understanding of the internet or plans for her future would do something that ignorant. Another standard that people don't expect from me is that I try to keep my language relatively clean. Sure, I'm not perfect and if pushed too hard, I drop an occasional F-bomb, but for the most part I try to rely on my vocabulary — without four letter words. And, thanks to the fine example of my parents and grandmother — not! — I have mostly remained clean and sober. Mostly.

Anyway, during the weekend, it became fairly obvious that Terrence assumed I was his 'girlfriend,' AKA bootycall. But the more I ignored his texts the more determined he became. And as his texts grew more rude and lewd and crude, I became more convinced — I really was done with him and couldn't wait to cut him loose. Now, I'd never admit this to Gloria, but I suppose I was still chewing on what she'd said about respecting myself. I wasn't sure it was even possible to truly respect myself, but whether I liked it or not, she'd got me thinking. After all, if I didn't respect myself, how could I expect anyone else to?

Something weird happened this morning. As I was in the bathroom, meticulously applying a second coat of mascara and reminding myself that I felt more power and confidence when I looked my best, I suddenly remembered being a little girl and how I watched my mom doing this exact same thing. I stopped and stared at the image in the mirror, startled to realize how much I resembled her. Same thick long auburn hair, which was even about the same length as hers when she died. Same sea-green eyes, full lips, and straight nose. It was sort of eerie—almost like my mom was staring back at me. And then it was like I could hear Eli's question again, asking me about what my mom would think of me now. My hand was actually shaking as I put the mascara wand back into the tube. Maybe it really was time to do some reevaluating.

Did that mean I was completely done with sleeping around? Well, who could know such things for absolute certain? But I did know this, I was done with Terrence, and I was done with his stinking pickup too. That was why I'd taken extra care with my hair and makeup this morning, and why I'd put on a denim skirt that showed off my legs, and a pale blue t-shirt that showed off my curves. I planned to stand strong and proud when I told Terrence to take a hike. As I went outside to wait for him, I knew I looked hot—even before a car full of guys honked and whistled.

Terrence pulled next to the curb with a grim expression, like he was still smoldering from last night's rejections. But one look at me and his scowl quickly turned into a stupid grin. He leaned over to the passenger window. "Hey, babe. Looking good."

"Hello, Terrence," I said crisply. "Thanks for stopping, but I don't need a ride this morning."

"Huh?" The scowl returned. "What'd'ya mean—"

"I mean, we're through, Terrence. It's been fun, but the fun's come to an end and I just wanted to tell you to your—"

"You can't dump me!" He jumped out of his truck, rushing over to me with a furrowed brow and not for the first time I wondered if he ever washed his greasy hair. "What'd I do anyway?"

"Nothing." I forced a stiff smile. "It's not you, Terrence, it's me." Okay, it was cliché and not really true, but it was all I had.

His dark eyes burned holes in me as he stepped closer with what can only be described as a seriously menacing expression. "Hey, you don't get off that easy, babe," he said between his teeth. "You can't just dump me without any—" He stopped to the sound of a horn honking.

I glanced over my shoulder to see Jude's Mustang slowing down. Eli waved from an open window and Pete and Tommy looked on with interest from the backseat.

"Hey, Mag," Jude called out. "Whazzup?"

Keeping a wary eye on Terrence—I meekly waved to them. "Hey, guys."

"Everything okay?" Eli called out.

Before I could answer, Terrence stepped in front of me, blocking me from the Mustang in a very territorial way. "Beat it," he yelled over his shoulder. "We got this under control."

"Not so fast," I stepped around Terrence. "Hey," I called out, trying not to sound nervous. "Got room for one more in there?"

"Sure," Pete called back.

"Hold on, Mag." Terrence grabbed me by the forearm, squeezing it painfully tight. "You're not going anywhere!"

"Let go of me," I yelled.

"Better listen to her." Eli was suddenly out of the car with Pete right behind him. Meanwhile, Jude and Tommy started to cheer and jeer like this was about to become a spectator event.

"Yeah, let her go," Pete firmly commanded. He's a linebacker and looks like he could easily take Terrence.

"You guys better butt out of this!" Terrence swore at them. "I'm warning you!"

"Let go of me, you jerk!" I yelled into Terrence's face, twisting to break free from him. "I'm going with them."

"That's right. She's coming with us." Pete grabbed Terrence by his shoulder, giving him a hard shove, and suddenly the two of them were going at it, swinging and punching and swearing.

"Stop it!" I screamed at them. I didn't want this to turn into an incident where the cops would be called and I could be implicated. "Both of you—stop!" Then, just as Pete's fist sailed straight for Terrence's face, I grabbed Pete by the arm, jerking so hard that he missed. Then with Eli's help, we dragged Pete back to his car and shoved him in the front passenger seat. Eli and I jumped in back next to Tommy. Terrence, still swearing, ran after the car beating a fist into the trunk of Jude's Mustang and then the tires screeched down the street.

"Sorry about that," I said after we were safely away. "But thanks, guys."

"What was that all about?" Jude asked.

"I just told him I wasn't that into him anymore," I said lightly.

"He didn't take it too well." Eli chuckled.

"He's a hotheaded bully," I told him. "That's just one of the reasons I broke up."

"One of the reasons?" Eli's dark brows lifted slightly.

"Yeah . . . one of them." I turned away to avoid his gaze.

"Well, you're smart to dump him," Tommy told me. "Terrence is a loser." Tommy glanced at me with what almost seemed like interest. "You deserve better."

Suddenly the other guys were jabbing at Tommy, teasing him that he wanted me all for himself. And for all I knew, it could be true. After all, he's a guy. I turned back to Eli, curious as to his take on this since he was keeping his mouth closed. But his expression, as usual, was impossible to read. Maybe he was thinking about his dad.

"How're you doing?" I quietly asked him. "I mean I haven't talked to you since, you know, losing your dad and everything."

"I miss him. But I know he's in a good place."

I frowned. "How can you possibly *know* that?"

His lips curved into a smile, but there was sadness in his eyes. "Some things you just know . . . inside of you."

I made a forced laugh. "Yeah, right . . . are you a prophet or something?"

His brow creased as if considering this. "Something, I guess."

But it was too late to question him further because Jude was parking in the school lot and everyone started pouring out of the car. Tommy looked at me with concerned eyes. "Do you think Terrence will give you any more trouble?"

Despite being a meathead football player, I suspected this guy had a sensitive side. Or else he was just playing me.

"I don't know. Probably." I tossed him a flirty smile. "You wanna do something about it? Wanna become my new hero?" I jabbed Pete in the side. "Although I doubt anyone could do a better job of it than you did. Thanks, dude."

Pete's eyes lit up. "Hey, anytime, Mag. I'd like to totally rearrange that freak's zitty face."

"Pete," Eli put his hand on his shoulder. "Don't go looking for fights, man."

"I'm not looking. I'm just saying if Maggie needs it, I can—"

"Don't bother," I said lightly. "I can take care of myself." I made a half wink. "But thanks for the offer." I patted Pete's cheek then blew him a kiss.

"Anytime, sunshine," he called out.

I waved then turned away, striding toward school in a strut that says look-at-me, and I was pretty sure Pete was looking. Probably Tommy too. Maybe they all were. And, really, one of those guys wouldn't be a bad catch—not that I was looking to catch anything more than a ride. But I could do worse. Still, I reminded myself that I was taking a break from guys. At least for awhile. Because, like it or not,

Gloria had been right about something. Sleeping around had never brought me happiness . . . or self-respect.

CHAPTER FIVE

I could've been flattered that, after several days, Terrence still seemed unwilling to let me go, but when he laid into Eli on Friday, shortly after school let out, I felt seriously worried. Not so much for Eli's sake, although that was concerning enough. But Terrence was making a scene in the courtyard across from the administration office, and I really didn't want to get hauled into the principal's office again. I'd already explained my way out of the skirmish with Julie and her gang of thug chicks a few weeks ago, I wasn't sure I could concoct another believable story.

"Bug off," I yelled at Terrence as he pinned Eli against a post. "You're just a loser and a bully."

"I knew you dumped me for Eli," Terrence shouted into my face. "And now he's gonna pay."

"You're insane." I grabbed Terrence's t-shirt, twisting it into a knot as I tried to pull him off Eli. "Why don't you just hit him?" I said to Eli. "Let him have it?"

"Because Eli is nonviolent." Pete stepped in with a couple of his buddies right behind him. "But I'm not." Suddenly they were all going at it. But spotting a security guard jogging toward the noisy scuffle that was starting to draw a crowd, I decided to make myself scarce. Sure, I felt sort of bad as I hurried toward the bus stop, but self-preservation trumps guilt. Besides, it was my day to meet with Gloria and I didn't want to miss my bus.

Gloria was suitably impressed to hear that I'd been writing in my journal. And I watched as she made careful note of the fact that I hadn't been with a guy in more than a week. She almost seemed proud of me. And I realized that a good report from her could go a long ways in keeping me out of hot water if I landed in the principal's office again. Not that I planned to.

"I've been meaning to ask you about that." Gloria pointed her pen at my bare arm.

I'd forgotten about my tank top and that it exposed the tattoo on my bare shoulder. "Oh, that." I shrugged. "No big deal. I got it when I was fourteen. Used fake ID. But my grandma's fine with it." Okay, that last bit wasn't true, but Grams eventually drowned her disappointment in me with her buddy Jack.

"But what does it mean?" Gloria frowned. "A black heart. It seems so symbolic and, no offence, rather dismal and hopeless."

I considered lying, but then wondered why. Who was she going to tell anyway? "It's not really a black heart," I began. "It's just that I tweak it a little. You know, with a black Sharpie pen."

"What?" She was clearly confused.

"It's a broken heart. I guess that was symbolic at the time." I shrugged.

"Because your heart had been broken?"

"I guess." I looked away.

"Was there someone who specifically broke it? Or was it just life in general?"

"I could say it was just life in general," I admitted. "But there was a guy."

"Want to tell me about him?"

"Not really." I could still feel the pain of Tyler's rejection.

"Okay."

"It's not a unique story," I said with irritation, knowing there was no point in keeping it from her. Especially considering patient confidentiality laws. "I was fourteen and felt like I was in love with this guy. Tyler. And I thought he was in love with me. I wasn't technically a virgin." I sighed. "But you know about how I was molested as a kid."

She nodded. "So you weren't technically a virgin, Maggie, but you'd never had consensual sex. But that's kind of like being a virgin, don't you think?"

"I guess so."

"So you had your first consensual sexual experience with a boy you loved?"

"But after Tyler got what he wanted he dumped me."

She didn't look the least bit surprised.

"And then he went around bragging, telling everyone at school about it."

"So that was the beginning of your *reputation?*"

I just nodded. I didn't want to tell her about all the other guys that were suddenly lining up at my door—or how gullible I'd been about their less than honorable intentions.

"So you got the broken heart tattoo," she finished my story for me, "and now you hide the broken heart behind the black heart." She smiled sadly. "It makes perfect sense."

For the first time, I almost liked this woman. Then she looked at her watch and I knew it was time to go. But as I rode the bus home, I felt like something good had happened—or was about to. I wasn't even sure what, but I felt like it was related to some of the choices I'd been making recently. And I felt almost hopeful . . . but then the voice of doom started droning, chipping away at me.

Don't fall for it, Maggie. Gloria can't be trusted. No one can be trusted. Not even you. And don't be tricked, life is never going to get better. If you were really smart, you'd check out now. It's just going to be one big dead end. It'll all go up in a puff of smoke. Just wait, you'll see. It's hopeless.

I tried to ignore it, but when I got home to find Grams splayed across the living room floor, I suspected the voice was right . . . again. *It was hopeless.* I frowned at the empty Jack Daniel's bottle on the floor next to one of Gram's fuzzy pink slippers. A nearly full bottle with a glass tumbler was still on the coffee table. She'd obviously started her party early today. As I set the empty on the coffee table, I wondered what the special occasion had been, then vaguely wondered if this would become her new norm. Wasted 24/7. That'd be something to look forward to.

It wasn't that I'd never seen Grams passed out before, but not usually this early in the day and not usually splattered all over the matted down living room carpet. When she was this far gone, she normally tried to land in her bedroom, usually in or near her bed. I leaned down, checking to be certain she was still breathing. Satisfied that she was alive, I tossed an old afghan over her and started to leave.

You gonna leave that whisky there? What's wrong with you, Maggie? Don't you want to escape your problems just like Grams is doing? Come on, it's easy. Just a sip or two and you'll feel a lot better. All your cares will be washed away.

So I picked up the bottle and took it to my room, setting it on my dresser. As I sat on my bed, I stared at the amber-colored liquid. I wouldn't have to drink a lot. Just enough to give me a good buzz—take me away from this nasty place. As if to confirm this really was a bug-infested dump, I spotted something brown scurry across the floor, I grabbed a flip-flop and smashed the cockroach with a loud thud. My life sucks. Truly, truly sucks. And the voice was right. It's never going to get better. I reached for the bottle, pulled off the lid, but then—instead of swigging it—I carried the detestable stuff to the bathroom and flushed it down the toilet.

Stupid, stupid, stupid!

CHAPTER SIX

Grams was furious the next morning. *"You did what?"* she shrieked at me. After she'd futilely searched everywhere . . . and I got sick of hearing her whine and complain, I eventually confessed to dumping her whisky.

"It just seemed the responsible grownup thing to do," I calmly told her.

"I'm the grownup here," she growled.

"Could've fooled me."

"You don't understand." Her voice trembled. "I need that whiskey — it was my last bottle."

"It's killing you, Grams." I shouted. "Can't you see that?"

And then, just like she always does whenever I confront her about her alcohol consumption, Grams burst into tears—and as usual, I just couldn't take it. So I left. But without any real destination in mind, I found myself walking toward the beach. And then, seeing that the Surf Shop was open, I decided to go in. I'd only surfed a few times, but enough to know that I could be good at it. That is if I had a surfboard. And even though I can't afford to purchase one, I could pretend to be looking. And, suspecting that Eli would be working today, it seemed a good excuse to talk to him.

As I went out of the bright sunlight into the dimly lit shop, I could hear female voices talking and giggling in the back.

"Come on, Eli," a girl said seductively. "You know you want it. Just give in and we'll give you the ride of your life."

"Unless you're gay," another girl said. "But I don't think you really are."

"I told you to leave me alone," Eli said in a quiet but firm voice.

"Not until we give you a good time," the first voice said. "Come on, Eli. You can't pass this up."

As my eyes adjusted to the dim light, I could see the two of them. Amber and Heather, wearing their skimpiest bikinis, and running their hands over Eli like a couple of cheap whores.

"Go away!" Eli said more firmly. "Now!"

"Listen to him!" I pushed my way past a clothing rack to glare at the sluts. "Get the hell out of here before I call the cops." I waved my phone in the air like a threat.

Amber swore at me but Heather stepped away from Eli.

"Seriously," I said in a calmer voice. "Why don't you go find someone who doesn't care *what* kind of trash he sleeps with?"

"Like you?" Heather sneered.

"Unlike you ugly skanks, I don't have to go around *begging* for it." I grabbed Amber by the arm, jerking her away from Eli. "You tramps must be as stupid as you look. You know, you could be pressed with assault charges, trespassing too since you're obviously not customers." I waved my phone again. "And I'm a witness to the crime."

Heather tossed more choice words at me and Amber threw some F-bombs at both of us, but my warning must've worked because they both backed away from Eli.

"She probably wants him for herself," Heather taunted from the front door. "That slut just can't get enough."

"Yeah," Amber chimed. "Everyone knows Maggie will sleep with anything. You can have him, skank!"

"But don't get your hopes up," Heather shouted. "Everyone knows that Eli's gay! We just wanted to prove it." Then laughing like idiots, they exited the shop.

I looked at Eli, trying to gauge how he was taking this. But he simply pushed his tussled hair off his forehead and re-buttoned his shirt. "Well, that was awkward." His smile seemed uneasy but genuine.

"Hope I didn't interrupt anything," I said sarcastically.

He looked slightly amused. "Hey, I appreciate your timing."

"Why were they doing that anyway?" I turned my back to him, pretending to check out a rack of sunglasses.

"Who knows?"

"They just showed up out of the blue? Started coming onto you?" I persisted.

"Amber was flirting . . . but she does that a lot. When I made it clear that I wasn't interested, they both started in on me. Acting like it was all a joke, like they thought they were seducing a gay guy. You know how they can be. Great fun."

I turned to face him. "You're not, are you?"

"What?" He looked evenly at me.

"Gay."

"Would it matter?" He smiled, but his eyes looked sad.

"Not to me." I smirked. "I don't care."

For a few minutes neither of us spoke, I just continued poking around like I was a serious shopper.

"Looking for anything in particular?"

I tried to act nonchalant as I flipped through a rack of board shorts. "Just checking out your inventory."

"You like to surf?"

"Yeah." I nodded, probably a bit too eagerly.

"Cool." He nodded. "Good waves out there today. Planning to catch some?"

"I don't have a board." I stared longingly at a sleek blue board on the display rack.

"Why not?" He looked at me in a way that suggested he knew the answer.

I shrugged, unwilling to admit my true financial status. It'd take me a year to save up enough for that board. I could barely afford to rent a board at the moment.

"You know . . . we've got a couple of used boards out back that I need to move. You interested?" He tipped his head to one side, studying me.

"I might be . . . ." I shoved my hands into my cutoffs pockets then pulled them out to show they were empty. "Or not."

He laughed. "I mean we need to get rid of them. As in they're free."

"Seriously?" I blinked.

He nodded, heading for the back door. "Come on."

"This isn't just charity?"

"No way. But I'll warn you, Maggie, they're not great boards. You'll see." He led me through a small workroom where several boards appeared to be in various stages of progress and then outside, to an open work area where even more unfinished boards were lined up in racks against the wall. "Over here." He went over to a dumpster with two surfboards leaned against it. One board had a pretty cool paint job and actually looked good, but the other board looked like trash. I ran my hand over the smooth board with the nice finish, imagining myself on it, riding a curling blue wave — it made for a nice picture.

"I don't recommend that one, Maggie."

I frowned. "Why not? Looks good to me."

"Appearances can be deceiving." He began to explain about inferior foam and foreign companies that use cheap blanks and crappy stringers and bad rockers — he might as well have been speaking Russian. "This board might look good on the outside, Maggie, but it's a mess underneath."

I frowned at the attractive board. "Is this supposed to be some sort of metaphorical life lesson for me? Like *beauty is only skin deep?*" I hated it when Grams said that to me—as in hint-hint.

He chuckled. "Well, I guess it could be." He tapped the shiny board. "But the only thing this is good for is to hang on your wall—and just pretend you're a surfer."

I looked at the shabby beat-up board. "What about this?"

"This one definitely needs some work, but she's got good bones and I think there's a lot of life left in her."

"What do you mean *needs some work?*"

Now he started talking about resins and epoxy, explaining how I could sand it down, fill in the holes and reseal the whole thing. "It takes some time and elbow grease, but if you do it right, you'll have a first rate ride."

I studied the sad looking board. "You think it's really worth the effort?"

"Absolutely."

"Then why don't *you* do it?" I asked. "You guys sell used boards here."

"Because I already have plenty of high quality blanks to finish. Without my dad around, there's more than enough work around here. And space is a factor. If you want this board, it's yours. And I'll even coach you through the refinish process." He patted the board. "It could be a really good board."

"Okay." I nodded. "I'll take it." I picked up the board, tucking it under my arm. "Do you sell the epoxy and resin and whatever else it is I'll need?"

"Yep." He grinned. "See, even though the board's free, I'll still make some profit off you."

I told him I'd take my board home and come back with some cash to get some supplies, which hopefully wouldn't cost too much. Eli promised to give me a quick lesson on the steps of resealing then I hauled my sorry looking surfboard away. I was nearly home when I wondered if I was being duped . . . again. Maybe Eli was back at his shop laughing over how he just foisted the trash off on me. Maybe I was a total fool.

Of course, you're a fool! And if you think you can trust Eli, you're a total idiot. He just wants to reel you in — so he can sleep with you. But you want that anyway, don't you? So play this up, Maggie. Go for it! Have some fun with Eli. You can hurt him before he hurts you. Now that'd be fun!

CHAPTER SEVEN

To my relief, Grams was gone when I got home. Probably off getting another bottle of Jack to drown her sorrows. And, really, it was probably just as well since I wasn't eager for her to see me lugging this big old surfboard into our cramped apartment. Grams already complains my stuff takes up too much room in our tiny roach ridden 'home.'

Eager to escape before her return, I shoved my board behind a chair then grabbed my wallet from where I'd stashed it in the bottom of my dirty clothes hamper, which is smelling pretty ripe. It wasn't that I don't trust Grams — although I don't. But even worse, I don't trust the lowlifes who dwell in this neighborhood. We've only been here a few months and we've already been broken into twice. I extracted what little was in my wallet, hoping it'd be enough to at least get started.

With cash in my pocket, I hurried back to the Surf Shop. And then, between waiting on customers and shaping a plank, Eli coached me through the steps of properly restoring a surfboard. He just happened to have one in need of attention. "You learn more by doing," he told me.

And so I spent the day meticulously sanding and filling, curing the epoxy in the sunshine, and then sanding and filling again . . . until it was time for the first topcoat of resin. "Wow, I said as I admired the smooth top of the shiny blue and green board. I know it needs more coats of resin, but it looks so much better."

"Nice work." He nodded with approval. "You're a natural."

"And how about the free labor?" I teased.

"Not exactly." He handed me a shoebox. "I'm taking your work in exchange for these materials."

"Seriously?" I peeked inside to see he'd put in epoxy, resin, sandpaper.

"Yep. You did a great job on that board, Maggie. It's a fair trade."

"Maybe you should hire me." I was only partly kidding.

"Wish I could, but we're on a budget here."

"I get that." I thanked him and started to leave.

"I'm guessing it'll take you a few days to get it repaired and ready for paint." He walked me to the door. "Don't forget to apply the chemicals outside. Those fumes are toxic."

"Yeah, yeah, you already told me."

"And when it's ready for paint, come on back and pick your colors."

Feeling oddly hopeful, I headed home only to find my beat up surfboard looking sadly rejected outside the front door. I picked it up and took it inside. But it was obvious that Grams was in a full-blown snit. "Don't bring that garbage back in here!"

"It's not garbage. It's my surfboard and I plan to restore it."

"Not in my house, you won't."

"I thought I lived in this fleabag too." I glared at her then looked around for her whisky bottle, wondering how much she'd had. Obviously not enough to sedate her yet.

"Your junk already takes up too much room." She waved a hand around the cluttered living room—which held as much of her junk as mine. "I told you when we moved to Ventura—thanks to you getting kicked out of your last school — that you'd have to get rid of some stuff, Maggie. And here you come dragging in another great big piece of junk. We don't have room!"

"Then get a bigger place!" I yelled back. "I told you we needed a three-bedroom apartment in the first place, but did you listen?"

"We can't afford a three-bedroom!"

"Is that my fault?" Spying her bottle of Jack on the kitchen counter, I grabbed it up, waving it in her face like evidence. "If you didn't waste so much money on your freaking Jack-crap, we could probably afford a bigger apartment!"

"Give that to me — right now!"

"No!" I held it close to my chest. "You need to quit this garbage, Grams. It's gonna kill you!" That's when I noticed the orange price-tag stuck to the side of the bottle. "Are you freaking kidding me? This poison costs almost *twenty bucks?*"

"Give It To Me!"

"And you down one of these a day? Or is it two now? I lost count." I put my superior mental math skills to work — and despite my general non-swearing standards, I let a doozy fly. "Do you know that just one bottle a day adds up to six-hundred dollars a month?" I screamed in disbelief. "*Six-hundred!* That's more than seven thousand dollars a year! That's more than enough to get us into a three-bedroom apartment." I stared at her in disbelief.

"Give that to me, Maggie!" She held out her hand.

"No!" I raced for the bathroom. "I'm flushing it—"

"*No!*" She went after me, but not fast enough. I slammed and locked the door, leaning my back against it, feeling the thuds of her fists against the cheap door as she pounded on it. Her screaming quickly dwindled down to pathetic whining, begging me not to dump her precious whisky.

"Don't do it," she pleaded in a hoarse voice. "Please, Maggie, don't do it. *I need that.*"

"I don't care." I moved toward the toilet, removing the cap from the bottle.

"You don't understand," she sobbed. "You don't know *why* I drink."

"Why?" I asked without genuine interest, holding the bottle over the toilet, ready to pour the poison down.

"It's partly your fault," she declared. "Oh, it started with your mother—I couldn't control her either. But you're just as bad, Maggie." She pounded the door for emphasis. "No, that's not true. You're worse! Your mother never got kicked out of school like you did. I never had to move from my home because of *her*."

Okay, that made me feel guilty. Was Grams' extreme dependence on alcohol really my fault? Oh, I knew she'd always been a drinker, but I had to admit it had gotten steadily worse these past few years. And I knew I'd stressed her out.

"Do you think that was easy on me? To up and move like that? At my age? To leave my friends and neighbors? Just so you could have a fresh start? And what are you doing with this fresh start? You've already been in trouble at school. Who knows what's next?"

I considered this . . . I hated to admit it, but her words sort of made sense.

"Maggie?" Her voice sounded weak and weary. "Are you listening?"

"What?" I snapped.

"Please, give it back to me — *please*."

I really didn't want to give in, but felt defeated. It was true that my problems had disrupted her life . . . maybe I really was to blame.

"You can keep the surfboard," she offered in a pleasant tone. "Just give me the bottle, Maggie, and I won't say another word about the surfboard. I promise."

"Fine." I opened the door and shoved the detestable bottle into her grasping hands. "Go ahead, kill yourself with your poison," I yelled. "See if I care."

As I stormed to my room, I pulled out my phone. I was ready to call up a guy, *any guy*, and ask him to take me away from here. Take me anywhere—to do anything. I didn't care. What difference did it make anyway? I skimmed through my contacts, even tempted to call Terrence and knowing he'd come running, and then I stopped. How was that any different than what Grams did? She uses her bottle to escape—I use a guy. We're both wimps.

I put my phone away and took a few minutes to actually write this into my journal. And then I went outside to get my surfboard. I felt slightly numb as I brought it into my already crowded bedroom. But I opened my shoebox and got out the sandpaper and, starting with the biggest grade like Eli had shown me, I started to sand. Grateful for the distraction, I spent the rest of the weekend working on my board. And by Sunday night, it didn't look real pretty, but the surface was smooth. Skin deep . . . I thought as I leaned it against the wall. Ugly on the outside . . . but according to Eli, good on the inside. Just the opposite of me.

CHAPTER EIGHT

Eli was pleased to hear that my board was almost ready for paint. "And I even drew out a design on paper," I told him and Jude on Monday morning. "It's just random graphics — color and line."

"I'd like to see it," Jude told me.

I pulled the colored sketch out of my bag then suddenly felt self-conscious.

"Let's have a look." Jude reached for it and Eli looked on.

"Cool." Eli nodded approval. "I like it, Maggie."

"Maybe I shouldn't have used so much color." I frowned. "That might get expensive — I mean to buy all those different paint colors."

"Just bring your board to the shop," Eli told me. "You can paint it there."

"That intricate design looks like it's gonna take some serious time." Jude pointed at my sketch. "Need any help?"

I shrugged, unsure if I wanted his help.

"Jude's really good at airbrushing," Eli said. "If he offers his assistance, you should take it."

So it was settled, I'd meet the guys at the Surf Shop on Saturday morning and with Jude's help, hopefully get it painted in one day. It was probably silly—but having this project and these guys to help me with it—somehow it made me feel unexplainably hopeful. As I walked to the Math Department, I felt like this was the beginning of what could be a really good week . . . like my life was about to get better.

Don't fall for it! You know those guys are just using you—they'll betray you. Just like everyone else has done. Hurt them, Maggie, before they can hurt you. And you can do it—you're an expert at manipulating males. Use your skills to get them—get them first!

I wanted to scream 'shut up' to the voice. But that would just make me look crazy and, despite my brief flirtation with hope, I knew there were still plenty of haters around, girls eager to trip me up. How they'd laugh at me when I fell flat on my face. And by the end of the day, my feelings of hope had been replaced with harsh realities. Mostly at the hands of a few mean girls determined to torture me.

"Hey, Mag." Todd Hanson put one hand on my shoulder, placing the other on the locker next to me, essentially pinning me to my locker. "What's up?"

"Nothing." I narrowed my eyes at him. *Do you mind?*

"Just saying hey." His smile was sleazy and he leaned so close I could smell alcohol on his breath. What a boozer.

"Hey." I tried to squeeze past him. "Back off, dude."

"Why so unfriendly?" He touched my cheek. "You know you're a lot prettier when you smile, Mag."

I pushed his hand away. "Bug off!"

He grinned. "Ooh, I like a feisty woman." His grip on my arm tightened.

"Seriously." I attempted a softer approach. "I want to go home and you're in my way."

"Oh, come on, Mags." He leaned his face close to mine. "You saying you don't wanna have some fun with me? I've got a case of beer in my car. We could hang at the beach and have—"

"What the hell?" Heather seemed to appear from nowhere, with Amber right behind her.

"Hey, Heather." Todd's hands flew to his sides as he stepped back, acting innocent.

"What's going on?" Heather glared at me.

"Nothing's going on." I turned to go, but Heather grabbed my arm, shoving me up against my locker, with Amber by her side.

"You putting the move on my guy?" she demanded angrily.

"Who can blame her?" Todd said in a teasing tone. "I'm hard to resist."

"Yeah, right." I rolled my eyes. "You can have your guy, Heather. That is if you can keep him." I faked a laugh. "But you might need a leash."

"You're such a pathetic slut!" Heather slapped me hard across the face and before I could return the favor, Amber grabbed my other arm.

"Two against one?" I yelled at them. "Real fair."

"Shut up, slut." Amber snarled. "And keep your skanky hands off our guys—"

"Gladly!" Determined not to engage in a fight that would get me into trouble, I just stood my ground. "Now take your skanky hands off of me."

"I'm not done." As Heather raised a fist, I braced myself for another blow, but when it came straight for my face, I ducked. Her hand slammed into the locker behind me and I couldn't help but laugh as Heather started swearing up a blue streak. But now Amber was getting ready to lay into me — and then Pete stepped in.

"Ladies, ladies." He spoke in a mockingly pleasant tone as he pushed Heather aside and tugged Amber off of me. "I just saw Mr. Richards coming this way and unless you'd all like to explain this little brouhaha to him, I suggest you make yourselves scarce."

"For now!" Heather glared at me. "But this isn't finished, slut."

"Come on," Todd urged Heather. "Let's get out of here."

As Mr. Richards passed by, the three of them strolled off, laughing and joking like they hadn't just been acting like lowlife thugs. But now I was fuming — ready to hit something or just scream, but instead of losing it, I slammed my locker shut and stormed away.

Pete, followed by Eli, Jude and Tommy, caught up with me outside. "What was that all about?" Pete asked with curiosity.

"Nothing," I growled at him.

"Then why were Heather and Amber getting ready to beat the crap out you?" Pete persisted. "You're welcome, by the way."

"Thanks a lot," I replied in a snarky tone. "But I would've been fine."

Pete laughed. "Didn't look like it to me."

Still too mad to talk and my face stinging from Heather's slap, I ignored him as we all stood around Jude's red Mustang, watching as Jude opened the trunk.

"Well, you can thank me later," Pete grabbed a couple of bags out of the trunk, tossing one to Tommy. "We gotta get to football practice." He winked at me. "See ya later, Mag."

I just glared at him. And, okay, I knew none of that was Pete's fault and he'd probably just saved my bacon, but I was still too mad to act civil.

"Wanna ride?" Jude offered cautiously.

Despite my rage, a ride sounded good, but I wasn't ready to admit it.

"Come on, Mag." Jude nudged me with his elbow. "We're your friends."

I turned to look at Jude and Eli. "Really?" I frowned with doubt. *"Friends?"*

"Looks like you could use some friends." Jude got into the driver's seat.

"Whatever." But instead of arguing, I got into the backseat, and trying to shake off my anger and indignation, I tried to act nonchalant.

"So what happened?" Jude glanced back at me as he started his car. "Why were those girls going to beat you up?"

I let out a long sigh then quickly explained about Todd hitting on me. "It's not the first time," I admitted. "And I'd already told him to get lost, but Heather showed up and threw her usual hissy fit." I poked Eli in the shoulder, remembering how those same girls pulled that stunt with him. "What's wrong with those girls anyway?"

He just shrugged.

"How can you be so nonchalant?" I demanded. "What about what they did to you on Saturday? That was practically—"

"What happened?" Jude asked with interest.

"It was nothing," Eli said quietly.

"*Nothing?*" I demanded. "They were attacking you, Eli."

"Huh?" Jude turned to look at me. "What did they do to him?"

So I explained about their sleazy seduction attempts, but Jude just laughed.

"Man, I wish I'd seen that." Jude shook his head.

"Aren't you mad at them?" I asked Eli.

"No," he said calmly.

"Why not?" I raised my voice. "Eli, they were all over you—and they were saying humiliating stuff. And yet you just act like it's no big deal. How can you just take it like that? I'd like to kill both of them! Seriously, I wish they'd both just drop dead. I would be so happy—I would dance on their graves."

"No, you wouldn't," Eli said quietly. "Not really."

"Yes, I would!" I shouted at the back of his head. "If I could murder them both and get away with it, I would—that's the God-honest truth!"

"I thought you didn't believe in God." Eli turned around to peer curiously at me.

"I don't! It's just a saying! A stupid saying." I could feel myself getting angrier by the second. "It doesn't mean anything. The point is—I wish that Amber and Heather were dead."

"And how does that make you feel?" Eli asked as Jude stopped for a traffic light. "I mean how are you feeling right now, Maggie?"

"Furious! Enraged!"

"Does that feel good — does it make you happy?"

His question made me want to hit something. "Of course not! *I'm furious!*"

"You want to feel better?" he asked as the car pulled out. "Do you *want* to be happy?"

"Like that's even possible." My hands were still balled into fists and I could feel my heart pounding in anger.

"Let it go, Maggie," he said gently. "That's the way to feel better."

"Let it go?" I shrieked. "Seriously?"

Eli just nodded, turning his back to me again.

"How?" I demanded. "How do you let crap like that go?"

"By forgiving," Eli said simply.

"Right." I rolled my eyes. "That'll happen."

No one spoke for a while, but as Jude pulled up to my apartment complex, I still wasn't ready to let this go. "Seriously, Eli, how is that even possible? I want to kill those girls — how do you expect me to forgive them? You might as well tell me to fly to the moon!" I got out of the car. "Because no way in hell am I gonna forgive those two witches. They don't deserve it!" I slammed the door.

Eli got out of the car and looked evenly at me. "You're probably right, Maggie." He just nodded.

"I'm right?" I stared at him in wonder. "Seriously?"

"Heather and Amber don't deserve to be forgiven by you. And neither does your grandmother."

"You are so freaking weird!" I yelled at him. "Eli Shepherd, I swear you are the weirdest guy on the planet!"

"I gotta second that motion," Jude joked from behind the wheel.

"Thanks for the ride," I told Jude. Then, still feeling irked from head to toe, I stormed up to the apartment. Eli is delusional—he seriously needs to get his head examined!

CHAPTER NINE

W hy is it that as soon as I attempt to respect myself, everyone else seems determined to drag me through the mud?" I couldn't believe I'd actually voiced this question to my therapist on Friday, but there it was just hanging in the air. But I had good reason to feel like this. Ever since Monday's attack by Heather and Amber, it had turned into a get-Maggie fest. It felt like those two girls had managed to turn every female at Kennedy High against me.

"Elaborate on how you've tried to respect yourself," Gloria gently prodded.

I was tempted to dish some BS, but didn't. "So . . . I was trying to take your advice, you know, with guys. And FYI

I haven't had *casual sex*—as you like to call it—for about three weeks. Maybe more. It's not like I count the days. I mean I'm not in some freaking twelve-step program."

"Maybe you should."

"Do a twelve-step program?"

"Count the days, Maggie. It might be interesting to see how long you can keep this going." Her smile looked authentic. "I'm proud of you."

I shrugged.

"So, who's dragging you through the mud?" she asked.

"Mostly girls."

"Calling you names and whatnot?"

"Yeah, *and whatnot.*" I nodded glumly. "It's pretty much nonstop and seems to be intensifying." I described Heather and Amber's recent attack, and how I've really been watching my back.

"Doesn't your school have an anti-bullying policy?"

I can't help but laugh. Seriously? Does she honestly think any schools enforce those policies? Get real!

"Have you reported the girls?"

I shook my head no. "It's useless. I mean these girls are so super good at this stuff. The little hypocrites act all sweet and nice when grownups are around, but tear into girls like me when backs are turned. And, even if it ends up in a brawl, I'm the one who'll get blamed."

"So you avoid them?"

"I try to, but it feels like there's a big target on my back."

"Why do you think they go after you so hard?"

"Because they're insecure witches who need to get a life?"

She smiled. "You're a very smart girl, Maggie. And you're a very pretty girl. Whether you can see it or not, I'm sure those girls feel jealous of you. You're right to call them insecure. I'm sure they are. One tactic that insecure people sometimes resort to . . . is to attack what they perceive as a threat. In other words, *you*."

I rolled my eyes. "You honestly think they feel threatened by the school slut?"

"Is that what you call yourself?"

"No, but they do."

"Well, you gave them that stone, Maggie. You told me yourself that you were sleeping around a lot. Maybe it's the only thing they have to throw at you. Of course, they're going to use it."

I let out a long weary sigh.

"But if you take that stone away from them — if you quit sleeping around and show yourself the respect you deserve, they won't have it to throw anymore."

"You make it sound so simple." I skeptically shook my head. "But you don't know these girls."

"That's true. So do you want to know the good news?"

"I could use some good news."

"In a couple of years this will all be behind you. If you can keep your grades up like you've been doing . . . and keep your nose clean . . . you'll probably be in college and these days will just be a memory."

"College seems so far away." I didn't want to admit that the mere idea of covering college tuition was overwhelming. Like I was dreaming the impossible dream.

"Don't give up, Maggie." She looked at her watch.

I thanked her and left, but as I walked to the bus stop, I didn't feel encouraged. Everything about my life felt hopelessly hard . . . like I could never escape it . . . never find my way.

That's right, stupid. You won't find your way. You can't — because it doesn't exist. So why keep trying? You're just beating your head against the wall. Can't you see that? Just give up. Go back to your old ways. And while you're at it, go see if you can pull Eli along with you. Because he's into you, Maggie. He wants you. You're the only girl that's turned his head. It's a

Friday night – go get him. He's lonely. He needs you – just like you need him. Go for it!

By the time I got home, I was seriously considering the voice of doom's advice. I mean what did I have to lose? Pretty much nothing. As I went up the rickety metal stairs to our apartment, I put together a plan. I would call Eli and ask about the writing I'd recently found on the bottom of my surfboard. I was honestly curious about it, wondering if it was important, or if I should just sand it off and cover it up. After we talked about that for a while, I would ask Eli about giving me surfing lessons. I'd heard he was pretty good. I could imagine the two of us out on the same board . . . the way I would entice him . . . the fun we could have. Oh, sure, Gloria would be disappointed . . . but really, what difference did it make? I reached for the doorknob, knowing that my recent record for not sleeping with guys would be broken tonight. And I didn't care. What difference did it make?

"Maggie." Grams opened the front door with a big smile. "I was hoping that was you. Come in, come in."

I frowned as I entered the apartment, trying to figure out what was up. "Is something wrong?" I tossed my bag onto the couch and stare curiously at Grams. Everything about this felt strange . . . creepy.

"Not at all."

I glanced around the apartment, which looked surprisingly clean. To add to the Twilight Zone sensation, a savory aroma wafted out of the kitchen. "Is someone coming for dinner?" I asked.

"Just you and me." She smiled, but her hands were trembling.

"What's going on?" I studied Grams closely. "You seem, uh, different." I wanted to say, 'who are you and what have you done with my grandmother?' but didn't want to hurt her feelings.

"I am different." She pointed to a chair. "Sit down. I want to explain."

Feeling seriously confused, I sank into a chair, waiting.

"Your words about my alcohol use got to me." Her eyes seemed unnaturally sparkly. "So I quit."

"You quit?" Okay, I was already feeling skeptical. "Seriously?"

"Yes." She nodded firmly. "I quit drinking."

"When did all this happen?"

She looked at the clock on the wall. "Well, let's see. It's been almost twenty-four hours now." She was literally wringing her hands and I could see beads of sweat on her brow.

"Twenty-four hours?" I repeated this, trying to wrap my head around this. "And you haven't had a single drink?"

"Not one. Yesterday I told myself that was the end. I was quitting."

"I admire your willpower, Grams . . . ." I wanted to add, *but I doubt it will work.*

"And I went to my first AA meeting this morning."

"Good for you." Okay, maybe she was serious. "How are you feeling?"

Her smiled faded slightly. "Well, I'm happy about quitting. I really am. But the truth is, I don't feel too good right now, Maggie." She leaned back in the chair with a sigh. "I was doing okay when I cleaned house. And then I made us dinner, but I really don't feel like I can eat. My stomach is a little queasy right now."

"Oh." I peered curiously at her. Her skin seemed paler than usual and those shaky hands had me worried. "Do you think it's safe to do stop drinking like this—I mean cold turkey? Should you see a doctor or something?"

She waved a hand. "No, no, I'll be fine. Oh, I've heard it can be a little rough at first. But the important thing is that

I *want* to do this. I *need* to do this." She slowly stood, moving toward the kitchen. "I'm doing it for—for both of us, Maggie. I—I—" She stopped talking and I could see she was sort of weaving back and forth. I was just going over to her when she collapsed onto the kitchen linoleum.

"Grams!" I stared down at her, watching in horror as she went totally rigid and began to jerk uncontrollably. I'd never seen a seizure, but I felt certain she was having one now. I fell to my knees, holding her close, trying to stop her from shaking, but seeing her eyes roll back in her head and her lips turning blue, I reached for my phone and with trembling fingers dialed 9-1-1.

CHAPTER TEN

My heart was still racing as I paced back and forth in the ER waiting room. All I knew was that I was right—Grams had suffered a seizure. "Probably from quitting alcohol without proper detox treatment," a female medic had explained as Grams was being loaded into the ambulance. "People can die from this."

That was all I could think about as I waited for someone to tell me how Grams was doing—*she could die from this!* And if she died, I would blame myself because I had ragged and ragged her—calling her names and nagging her to quit drinking. So then she does—and now this? Wasn't it my fault?

It was around six o'clock and I just couldn't take it anymore. I went to the receptionist, demanding that either someone talk to me or I'd go back there and find out for myself. "Just a minute," she said quickly.

Before long, a doctor emerged with a solemn expression. "Your grandmother is in critical condition," he said stiffly. "She's in ICU right now. We won't know anything for certain until we run some scans and tests."

"When will that be?"

"After she's stabilized." He glanced down the hallway behind me. "I'm sorry I can't tell you more. You'll just have to be patient."

"Is she going to die?" I demanded.

He seemed to be weighing his response. "We're doing everything we can to prevent that." He reached over to place a hand on my shoulder. "But if you're a praying person, well, you probably should do that." Then he excused himself and left.

A praying person? Seriously? That was his best advice? He obviously had no idea that, not only was I not on good terms with God, but that I didn't believe any of that crap. Even so, I found myself walking down to a small room that I'd noticed earlier. With stained glass windows, a few pews and some sort of altar, I assumed it was a religious place. Not that I'd had much experience with such things. But taking the doctor's words to heart, I went into the room and sat down. But to pray? Where would I even begin?

As desperate as I felt, I knew it was hopeless. What was I supposed to say? Like *hey, God, I don't believe in you, but could you do me a favor?* Seriously? It sounded hypocritical—and if there were a God, I suspect it would be insulting. And so I left, but before returning to the ER waiting room, I called the Surf Shop. I didn't even know if Eli would be there, or what I'd say if he was—but for whatever reason, he seemed the right person to call.

"Surf Shop," he answered brightly.

"Eli?" I said in a raspy voice.

"Maggie? Are you okay?"

"Not—not really." My words poured out in a jumbled mess as I attempted to explain about Grams' alcoholism and quitting cold turkey and how it'd caused a seizure. "I'm afraid she's dying—and the doctor said to *pray*." My voice cracked. "But I—I honestly don't know how." I was crying now. "And I—I thought maybe you would know how. I mean I don't really know if you're religious, but I remember that time with Savannah's dog and you seemed—oh, I don't know." I collapsed into sobs.

anced
"Jude is here at the shop with me," Eli said. "But we were just closing up. How about we swing by the hospital, Maggie?"

"Really? You'd do that?"

"Yeah. See ya in about twenty minutes."

As I pocketed my phone, I wondered what good it would do to have Eli and the guys here at the hospital — and yet I felt comforted to think I wouldn't be alone. And, really, as pathetic as it is to admit, Grams and I don't have anyone. No family and no close friends . . . no one to really turn to. And if I lost her, well, I didn't want to think about that — but I would blame myself.

It's your fault when she dies. You goaded her into quitting alcohol. She did it for you. And now you'll lose her and you'll be alone . . . or worse, you'll be back in the foster care system. Why don't you do the world a favor, Maggie? Just go to the top floor of the hospital and take a flying leap. It won't hurt much. And no one will miss you. All your troubles will be over and your pain will be gone. End of story.

As I walked back toward the little religious room, I was tempted by the voice of doom's words. That really would be an easy way out. Why not just put an end to all this suffering? No one would care. Well, unless Grams survives. She might care. If she survives.

I sat down on the back bench and tried to think of a prayer, but the only words that came to me were: "Oh, God. Oh, God. Oh, God." And that didn't seem much of a prayer, but it was all I had.

"Maggie?" I turned to see Eli, followed by Jude, coming into the room. "How is she?" Eli asked as he slid in beside me. Jude slipped into the row in front of me. They were both looking on with what seemed genuine sympathy and concern—and I suspected Eli had filled Jude in about Gram's alcohol addiction and the cause of her seizure.

"I don't know," I told them.

"Are you praying?" Jude asked.

I shook my head. "I really don't know how."

"Eli knows how," he said. "Don't you, Eli?"

"There's not much to it." Eli shrugged. "You just say what's on your mind . . . to God . . . and believe that he's listening. That's all."

"Will you—will you pray for my grandma?" I whispered.

Eli pursed his lips then closed his eyes and, not wanting to stare at him, I closed my eyes too. But no one said anything. We all just sat there for several minutes and finally Eli mumbled what sounded like 'amen.' I opened my eyes and stared at him.

"Are you done?" I asked.

He just nodded.

I felt confused, but resisted the urge to ask 'is that all there is to it?' Instead, I thanked him, thanked them both, and stood.

"I hope she's okay," Jude said.

"I better go check with the receptionist," I said nervously. "To see if anything has changed." I went to the receptionist, making my inquiry, but after making a call, she glumly shook her head. "Nothing's changed. They say she's still in critical condition. Still unconscious."

"Oh . . . ." I swallowed against the lump building in my throat, wondering what I'd expected. Did I think that Eli's prayer was going to save her? Was I really that naïve and foolish? I could hear the voice of doom condemning me for my stupidity, but I tried not to listen. The guys were coming over to join me in the waiting area.

"How is she?" Jude asked quietly.

"The same." I blinked back tears, trying to appear strong.

"I hate to take off like this." Jude nodded to the clock and I was surprised to see it was a little past seven. "But I promised to be home in time for my sister's birthday party. And I'm already a few minutes late."

"I understand," I said quickly. "And I'm sure my grandmother will be just fine." Okay, that was a big fat lie. But what right did I have to keep them around? I assumed Jude had driven Eli—and that he needed to take him home. "Thanks for coming, guys. I really appreciate it." I forced what I hoped was a brave smile.

"Let us know how she's doing." Eli held up his phone. And then we said goodbye. As soon as they left, I broke down into tears. I'd never felt so alone or scared . . . never. It was like this really was the end of my rope. Like if Grams died, I would be totally out of options. I couldn't go back into the system . . . I'd rather take a flying leap off the top floor of the hospital. In fact, I decided—if Grams didn't make it, that is just what I would do. Call it a day. End of story.

That's when I noticed some little kids staring at me, probably wondering why I was such a blubbering mess. So I hurried to the restroom, tossed cold water onto my face, and tried to get a grip. I was just coming out when I saw the doctor coming down the hallway toward me.

"There you are," he said. "Your grandmother is awake and wants to see you."

"Really?" I felt a rush of hope as I followed him. "She's okay?"

"Yes. She regained consciousness about twenty minutes ago," He explained as we walked. "I examined her, and she seems to be in surprisingly good condition, all things considered. She even knew what day it was. But I still want to run more tests and she'll need to remain hospitalized for a few days. Until she's thoroughly detoxed from alcohol, but I'd say the prognosis is good."

As we went past the receptionist's desk, I glanced up at the clock. Twenty minutes ago must've been about the same time Eli had prayed for Grams. Was it possible . . . was God really listening?

Eli and Jude seemed somewhat surprised when I showed up at the Surf Shop the next morning. "I told you she was better last night," I reminded Eli as I leaned my surfboard against the wall by the door. "I spent the night at the hospital and would've stayed all day. But Grams told me it was a waste of time for me to sit and hold her hand. She insisted I should go out and get some fresh air." I smiled. "And I didn't argue with her."

"So she's really gonna be okay?" Jude asked.

"The doctor sounds pretty positive." I looked curiously at Eli. "He told me that she regained consciousness around seven o'clock last night," I said carefully. "Right about the same time you were praying for her."

"What a coincidence." Eli turned his focus onto my surfboard, studying it closely.

"How long will she be in the hospital?" Jude asked.

"Until she's done detoxing—four or five days."

"Do you think she'll really quit drinking for good?" he asked.

"I sure hope so. She claims that she's done with it. I think having that seizure might've sealed the deal for her."

"So maybe it was for the best." Eli ran a hand over the top of my surfboard. "This feels really good, Maggie. Nice work. And you were right—it's ready for paint."

"But what about the words on the back of it?" I asked Eli.

"Words?" Eli picked up the board, laying it face down on the work table. "What words?"

I pointed to the spot where I could barely make out some letters. "It looked like the letter B and O. And then like Stein-something."

"Bo Steinfeld?" Eli said with interest.

"No way," Jude grabbed a work light, holding it over the board to see better.

"It is!" Eli exclaimed. "Look. It's the real deal. It says *Bo Steinfeld.*"

"No way, dude!" Jude bent down to see better then slowly shook his head. "How did Maggie get so lucky?"

"Lucky?" I grimaced. "Seriously? Me?" I leaned over to peer at the words. "What does that mean? Who is Bo Steinfeld?"

"Just one of the greatest board shapers of all times," Jude told me.

Eli nodded solemnly. "Bo was a world class surfer in the 1960s. He got hurt riding the Beast in Hawaii back in the 1980s. Paralyzed from the waist down. But he still loved surfing and took up making boards. Really good boards."

"Man, Bo was the best." Jude put the light away.

"Bo was a friend of my dad's, the one who taught Dad all about shaping boards. Bo died when I was a kid."

"And this was his board?" I stared at the board in wonder.

"Well, probably not a board he personally used," Eli explained. "But he obviously made it—and it's valuable."

Now I felt guilty. "Then I should give it back to you, Eli. It's really yours. I don't want to—"

"No way." He firmly shook his head. "It's yours now, Maggie. You rescued it. You did the work on it. You gotta keep it."

"But if it's such a good board . . . so valuable . . . I don't know. Maybe you should keep it, Eli."

"Remember how it almost went in the dumpster?" Eli said.

"And how I almost took the other board," I reminded him, "thinking it was the better one—just because it looked good on the outside. But you encouraged me to take this one instead, said it had good bones." I ran my hand over the board. "But I had no idea it was this special."

"It's special because it has the maker's mark on it," Eli said solemnly. "But it was so beat up, we couldn't tell. But that's what gives it value, Maggie, *the maker's mark*." His face broke into a smile. "And I think Bo would be glad to know it's in such good hands too."

I felt a tiny wave of hope wash over me. "I'll take really good care of it," I promised Eli. "I won't let it get beat up or anything."

"You don't mean you'll just hang it on your wall?" Jude frowned with concern. "That'd be wrong."

"Yeah," Eli added. "Bo wouldn't approve of that, Maggie. This is board that's meant to be out there. It needs to catch waves. Bo would expect you to have a good time with one of his boards."

"Oh . . . okay," I agreed uneasily.

"We'll get it all painted and looking good and then you'll have to hit the surf, Mag." Jude set an airbrush and selection of paints on the work table. "And I wanna be there to see you hanging ten on Bo's board. That'll be cool."

"I have a confession to make," I admitted sheepishly. "I barely know how to surf." I watched their amusement. "I mean I've been out a few times on rental boards, but I'm not very good. And I'd never forgive myself if I did something stupid and ruined this surfboard."

"We'll teach you," Eli promised.

"Yeah," Jude agreed. "You seem like a gutsy girl to me, Mag. A few lessons and you'll be just fine."

"And this board is tough enough to take a beginner," Eli assured me. "Plus it's well-balanced. That'll help you get the hang of it."

As I worked on my surfboard, learning to use the airbrush and carefully painting the intricate design I'd drawn, I felt like this board and I had a few things in common. We'd both been a mess and people had assumed we were worthless, but we actually had value. Now if only had the maker's mark on me . . . I might be worth even more.

It was late in the day, and Jude and I were just finishing up my board, when I felt a fresh wave of hope wash over me. Even though I had no idea what lay ahead, I thought maybe I could face it . . . with friends like Eli around. And, sure, I could be wrong and I've been wrong before—but deep down inside of me I didn't think Eli could betray anyone. Not even someone like me. I felt like maybe, just maybe, I could trust him.

OTHER YA BOOKS BY MELODY CARLSON

Diary of a Teenage Girl series
True Colors series
Secrets series
Carter House Girls series

For more information, or to sign up for her newsletter, visit her website: melodycarlson.com

Visit

The Eli Diaries Site

—To read first chapters from each of the books before they are published.

—To watch interviews of the authors.

—To ask the characters, authors and Eli questions.

https://www.amarismedia.com/eli-diaries

CPSIA information can be obtained
at www.ICGtesting.com
Printed in the USA
LVHW03s1752220618
581593LV00002B/342/P